What Kids Say About
Carole Marsh Mysteries . . .

I love the real locations! Reading the book always makes me want to go and visit them all on our next family vacation. My Mom says maybe, but I can't wait!

One day, I want to be a real kid in one of Ms. Marsh's mystery books. I think it would be fun, and I think I am a real character anyway. I filled out the application and sent it in and am keeping my fingers crossed!

History was not my favorite subject until I starting reading Carole Marsh Mysteries. Ms. Marsh really brings history to life. Also, she leaves room for the scary and fun.

I think Christina is so smart and brave. She is lucky to be in the mystery books because she gets to go to a lot of places. I always wonder just how much of the book is true and what is made up. Trying to figure that out is fun!

Grant is cool and funny! He makes me laugh a lot!!

I like that there are boys and girls in the story of different ages. Some mysteries I outgrow, but I can always find a favorite character to identify with in these books.

They are scary, but not too scary. They are funny. I learn a lot. There is always food which makes me hungry. I feel like I am there.

What Parents and Teachers Say About Carole Marsh Mysteries . . .

I think kids love these books because they have such a wealth of detail. I know I learn a lot reading them! It's an engaging way to look at the history of any place or event. I always say I'm only going to read one chapter to the kids, but that never happens—it's always two or three, at least!
—Librarian

Reading the mystery and going on the field trip—Scavenger Hunt in hand—was the most fun our class ever had! It really brought the place and its history to life. They loved the real kids characters and all the humor. I loved seeing them learn that reading is an experience to enjoy! —4th grade teacher

Carole Marsh is really on to something with these unique mysteries. They are so clever; kids want to read them all. The Teacher's Guides are chock full of activities, recipes, and additional fascinating information. My kids thought I was an expert on the subject—and with this tool, I felt like it!
—3rd grade teacher

My students loved writing their own mystery book! Ms. Marsh's reproducible guidelines are a real jewel. They learned about copyright and ended up with their own book they were so proud of!
—Reading/Writing Teacher

"The kids seem very realistic—my children seemed to relate to the characters. Also, it is educational by expanding their knowledge about the famous places in the books."

"They are what children like: mysteries and adventures with children they can relate to."

"Encourages reading for pleasure."

"This series is great. It can be used for reluctant readers, and as a history supplement."

FANTASY
FIELD TRIPS

Adventure to the

PLANET MARS!

by Carole Marsh

Managing Editor: Sherry Moss
Senior Editor: Janice Baker
Assistant Editor: Mike Kelly
Cover Design: Vicki DeJoy
Cover and Inside Illustrations: Kirin Knapp (casuallygreen.com)
Content Design: Darryl Lilly, Outreach Graphics

Mars is a trademark of Mars, Incorporated.

Gallopade International is introducing SAT words that kids need to know in each new book that we publish. The SAT words are bold in the story. Look for this special logo beside each word in the glossary. Happy Learning!

Gallopade is proud to be a member and supporter of these educational organizations and associations:

American Booksellers Association

American Library Association

International Reading Association

National Association for Gifted Children

The National School Supply and Equipment Association

The National Council for the Social Studies

Museum Store Association

Association of Partners for Public Lands

2D Years ago...

As a mother and an author, one of the fondest periods of my life was when I decided to write mystery books for children. At this time (1979) kids were pretty much glued to the TV, something parents and teachers complained about the way they do about web surfing and blogging today.

I decided to set each mystery in a real place—a place kids could go and visit for themselves after reading the book. And I also used real children as characters. Usually a couple of myown children served as characters, and I had no trouble recruiting kids from the book's location to also be characters.

Also, I wanted all the kids—boys and girls of all ages—to participate in solving the mystery. And, I wanted kids to learn something as they read. Something about the history of the location. And I wanted the stories to be funny. That formula of real+scary+smart+fun served me well.

I love getting letters from teachers and parents who say they read the book with their class or child, then visited the historic site and saw all the places in the mystery for themselves. What's so great about that? What's great is that you and your children have an experience that bonds you together forever. Something you shared. Something you both cared about at the time. Something that crossed all age levels—a good story, a good scare, a good laugh!

20 years later,

Carole Marsh

Christina Mimi Papa Grant

Hey, kids! As you see—here we are ready to embark on another of our exciting Carole Marsh Mystery adventures! You know, in "real life," I keep very close tabs on Christina, Grant, and their friends when we travel. However, in the mystery books, they always seem to slip away from Papa and I so that they can try to solve the mystery on their own!

I hope you will go to www.carolemarshmysteries.com and apply to be a character in a future mystery book!

Well, The Mystery Girl is all tuned up and ready for "take-off!" Gotta go... Papa says so! Wonder what I've forgotten this time?

Happy "Armchair Travel" Reading,

Mimi

About the characters

Ms. Bogus' Fourth Grade
Alpine McAlpine School

Can you imagine a class where you go on field trips that are literally "out of this world?" The kids in Ms. Bogus' fourth grade class don't just imagine Fantasy Field Trips—they experience them!

Meet Ms. Bogus, the quirky teacher with the big heart and even bigger imagination! On the left are twins Skylar and Drew, and Colette, who sits in a wheelchair but stands tall in the middle of every Fantasy Field Trip adventure! On the right are Lucia, the girl who loves to travel; Willy, the class clown with lots of big ideas; and Sarah, the shy blonde who loves to read.

There are lots of other kids to meet in Ms. Bogus' class, too. So, let's go—it's time for a Fantasy Field Trip!

Books in This Series

Table of Contents

Prologue

The Alpine McAlpine school bus pulled off I-40 into Flagstaff, Arizona on its way to the Lowell Observatory. A sign on the side of the bus printed in big bold letters claimed, LOWELL OBSERVATORY OR BUST!

"The wheels on the bus go round and round, round and round, round and round, the wheels on..." Drew, Skylar, Willy, Colette, and Lucia sang at the top of their lungs.

Sarah, on the other hand, was doing what she usually did. She had her head buried in a book. Even though this book was older and a little more tattered than the usual science books she liked to read, she was enjoying its main theme, plus it had lots of pictures. Her only movement was to occasionally brush her blond hair away from her sapphire-blue eyes.

"Come on, Sarah," Lucia said. "Come and join us! You can read your book at the hotel tonight." Lucia gazed out the bus window at the sparkling streetlights. This was the first nighttime field trip the class had ever taken.

"You know I don't like to sing," Sarah said. "I have a terrible voice."

"My voice teacher says there's no such thing as a terrible voice," Lucia said, "just an untrained voice. Besides, we ran out of songs to sing, anyway."

"I don't know," Sarah said. "This is a really interesting book."

Lucia made a skeptical face. "Really?" she said. "What's the name of this really interesting book?"

Sarah held it up for Lucia to see. "The Mystery of the Face on Mars," she said.

"Okay, so what's the mystery?" Lucia asked. "And whose face is on Mars?" Looking over her shoulder, she added, "I hope it's not Willy's! "

Willy was showing Colette his favorite Martian face, by hooking his little pinky fingers in his mouth and pulling on his eyes with his forefingers to distort his face.

Sarah giggled. "No, the face isn't *that* bad," she said. "Back in 1976, the *Viking 1* spacecraft was orbiting Mars, snapping pictures of possible landing areas for another spacecraft. One of the pictures showed an eerie image of an enormous head almost two miles long. It seemed to be staring right at the spacecraft's camera."

"Interesting," Lucia said, obviously uninterested.

Willy plopped into the seat next to Sarah. "It's only interesting if the face blinked or fluttered its eyelashes or something," Willy said. "Otherwise, it's just a land formation like a mesa or a butte. Hey, maybe it's the face of the Roman god of war." Willy snapped his fingers as if trying to think of his name. "Oh! What's his name? Oh, yeah! Mars!"

"Very funny, funny boy," Sarah said. "The interesting part is that some people claim that NASA is involved in a cover-up. They say the face is too **symmetrical** to be naturally made, so it must have been made by aliens!"

"You mean there might really be Martians?" Lucia asked.

CHAPTER ONE

You're It!

Willy peeked around the exhibit he was hiding behind in the Lowell Observatory rotunda. He kept an eye out for his teacher, Ms. Bogus. She was tall, pear-shaped, and never went anywhere without the strand of white pearls that laid against the front of her oversized dress. Her short, unbrushed hair and outdated, slip-on shoes made her look quite old fashioned. But what really stood out were the cat-eye, gold glasses that were always perched low on her nose.

Ms. Bogus stood across the room at a display case, reading. Sarah leaned against the display case next to her. She was the only student not playing tag.

Willy couldn't see Drew, his twin brother Skylar, or Lucia, which was okay because they weren't "It." Colette was. Willy didn't like it when Colette was "It" because she was like a Ninja girl in a wheelchair. She was so quiet he couldn't hear her moving around. There were no feet shuffling or footsteps to listen for, so he had learned to look for her shadow, but right now he couldn't see it anywhere.

Willy slithered to the other side of the exhibit. He stuck his head out just a bit.

"You're It!" Sarah whispered, tagging Willy on his elbow from behind. He jumped.

Willy spun around, but Colette's wheelchair was already streaking away from him.

"Man!" Willy said. "She always manages to sneak up on me." He tucked his head into the arch of his bent arm as he leaned against the back of the exhibit. "One-one-thousand, two-one-thousand, three-one-thousand..."

Drew was hiding just 10 feet from where Willy had been tagged by Colette. As he took another bite of his Mars candy bar, he saw Willy tuck his head into his arm. Drew dashed quickly to another part of the observatory. He didn't have to worry, though—he knew Willy would be on the hunt for Colette. Willy hated getting tagged by Colette, so whenever it happened, he went right after her. Drew just had to be careful so that Willy wouldn't stumble upon him!

"Nine-one-thousand, ten-one-thousand! Watch out everybody, here I come," Willy called. He peered in the direction Colette had gone. The path took him right past Ms. Bogus. As he quietly tiptoed past her, he saw a partially open door on the side of the main rotunda.

"Willy," Ms. Bogus said, without even looking over her shoulder at him, "you're going to have to wind up your game of tag soon, because we have a presentation to attend."

"Uhh!" Willy gulped. "Okay, Ms. B."

Willy squeezed through the doorway, quietly shutting the door behind him. It was dark, very dark. "This is a perfect place for Colette to be hiding," he thought. He took out his cell phone and opened it for just a few seconds. The light emitting from the little screen gave him a quick view of his surroundings.

It was time for Willy to become a Ninja himself. He set out slowly and quietly, like a jungle cat hunting its prey. He emitted no sound, except for his quiet, slow breathing. Stealth was everything in a good game of

"You're It." He got down on his hands and knees and crawled further into the dark void, feeling around, hoping to accidentally touch Colette.

He bumped into something hard. He patted the floor around it. It was a table with some sort of machine on it. The machine felt like a projector they used in school to show movies. He kept crawling. He could hear people talking, but he couldn't make out what they were saying.

Ms. Bogus stood outside the double doors that led into the Vickers McAllister Space Theatre. She peered over the top of her glasses, as the children lined up to go inside. She noticed Willy was nowhere in sight.

"Does anyone know where Willy is?" Ms. Bogus asked the class.

Drew tried to cover for him, wrapping a loose strand of long blond hair behind his ear. "I think he went to the bathroom, Ms. B."

"I'll go fetch the lad," a museum worker offered. "In the meantime, you can get the other children situated inside." He strolled to the doors and stopped. "Children, there is to be no talking beyond this point. Find yourself a seat and the presentation will start shortly." He opened the doors for them to enter and then headed toward the Men's Room.

The children sat in the front of the room. No one uttered a word as they watched the back door for Willy.

Willy muttered to himself as he continued to crawl. "If there was just a little bit of light, I could see if I'm on the right track," he said. His left shoulder bumped into a corner. He felt around it and decided it must be the entrance to another room. He followed the wall around the corner and stayed close to it as he slid further into the darkness. This has got to be where she's hiding, Willy thought.

The lights in the theater dimmed slowly. The children turned back toward the heavy black curtains in front of them as they began to part. Suddenly, they all burst into laughter as they saw Willy, on his hands and knees, below the projection screen.

Willy stared out into the sea of laughing faces. He stood up and wiped off his pants. "I was wondering when you guys were going to get here," he said with a red-faced grin. He bowed and made a circular motion with his arm. "I now present...the planet Mars!"

Just as Willy said, "Mars," an image of Mars burst onto the screen behind him.

The theater filled with wild applause!

CHAPTER TWO

Donuts for Everyone

Dr. Bob Parker stood at the front of the theater. A laptop computer was perched on top of the podium next to him. Ms. Bogus had just introduced him as one of the research scientists who worked at the Lowell Observatory. He typed in a few computer commands and Mars came into sharper focus on the screen.

"This is the planet Mars," Dr. Parker said. "At the moment, it is 40 million miles from earth." An image of the earth and Mars orbiting the sun appeared, splitting the screen.

"That mileage varies because of Mars' further distance from the sun and its elliptical orbit, as you can see here," Dr. Parker explained, pointing at the screen with a red laser pointer. "Does anyone know how long it takes the earth to make one orbit of the sun?"

Everyone raised their hands. Willy was one of the last to do so. Dr. Parker looked at his nametag. "Willy, what do you think?"

"That's easy," Willy replied, squirming in his seat. "I know the answer to this because I've watched my older sister fix her hair and put on makeup, and by the time she was done, all four seasons had come and gone," Willy said. The other boys snickered. "It takes 365 days or one full year," he finally answered.

"That's right, Willy," Dr. Parker said. "So then, does anyone know how long it would take Mars to make one orbit of the sun?"

Sarah was the only student to raise her hand. "What's the answer, Sarah?" Dr. Parker asked.

"Like Willy said, that's easy," she answered. "It's 687 earth days or four times longer than it takes Willy to get a school project done!"

"Hey!" Willy said. "That was a really hard project."

Everyone giggled.

"You're correct, Sarah," Dr. Parker said.

"Is that a live image of Mars?" she asked.

"Yes," Dr. Parker said. "It's being relayed to us by NASA's Mars Reconnaissance Orbiter that is currently in orbit around Mars."

"If the gravity on Mars is less than on Earth, would things weigh less?" Colette asked in a soft voice.

"Good question, Colette," Dr. Parker said. "How much do you think your dad weighs?"

"I'm not sure, but my mom says he weighs too much, and that he's got to stop going to the donut shop when he's working," Colette said.

"I didn't know your dad was an Alpine policeman!" Willy said, grinning. The rest of the class giggled.

"He's not, Mr. Smarty Pants," Colette said. "He's an insurance salesman, and his office is right next to the donut shop." Colette turned back to Dr. Parker. "I think I heard him say he weighs 180 pounds."

"Very good," Dr. Parker said, writing 180 on a marker board next to the podium. He then divided it by 2.6. "On Mars, your dad would weigh about 69 pounds," he explained. "Everyone, pull out a piece of paper and write your weight on it. Then, divide your weight by 2.6. Your answer is your approximate weight on Mars."

"Wow!" Drew said. "I'd weigh less than 40 pounds. Man, I bet I could jump pretty far on Mars."

"Yes, you could, Drew," Dr. Parker said.

Skylar raised his hand. "Are there really aliens on Mars?" he asked.

"We don't believe there are," Dr. Parker said. "We haven't found proof of any life on Mars yet, at least not anything above microscopic life."

Not to be outdone by his brother, Drew threw his hand up. "I thought I read a display that Percival Lowell found irrigation canals on Mars built by an intelligent civilization."

"Well, Drew, you did," Dr. Parker said, "but the rest of that display went on to explain how Percival was wrong. The canals he saw were just an optical illusion. Remember, back then we didn't have probes that could go to Mars and take pictures. The first photographs we got back from the *Mariner 4* space probe in 1965 proved there weren't any canals."

Tap, tap, tap.

The children turned in the direction of a light knock on the back doors of the theater. A tiny, gray-haired woman entered quietly, carrying a brown box. She handed the box to Ms. Bogus, whispered something in her ear, and then hurried out of the room. Ms. Bogus set the box on the table next to her.

"What's in the box?" Willy asked. "I hope they're donuts!" The class giggled.

Colette gave him her best "Shut Up!" stare.

"Hey," Willy said. "I'm really hungry."

CHAPTER THREE:

Mars-velous

"What about the Face on Mars?" Sarah asked Dr. Parker. "Some people believe it was built by intelligent beings that passed through our solar system. Is NASA hiding the truth about the face?" she continued. "I think the image taken by our *Viking 1* spacecraft in 1976 looks too symmetrical to be a natural landform like a mesa or a butte. What do you think it is, Dr. Parker?"

"I believe it's just a natural landform," Dr. Parker replied, as he typed in several commands on the laptop. "This is the area of Mars we call Cydonia. It's where the Face on Mars is located. And this is what Sarah is talking about."

The screen split in two, with the *Viking 1* photograph of the Face on Mars on the left, and a real-time image on the right.

"Wow!" Willy said. "That looks like the face of one of those Egyptian pharaohs. That is one homely guy!"

"The picture on the left is the one that caused the big stir—it's two miles long," Dr. Parker explained. "Let me close in on the real-time face on the right of the screen." His fingers flew over the keyboard and the Face on Mars grew to fill the screen.

"That does look like something someone created," Sarah said.

"Naw!" Willy said with a snort. "You can see the valleys where the eye sockets are, and the part that looks like a nose is just a mountain. Besides, have you ever seen a building that size? That's bigger than the pyramids and the Pentagon put together!"

"That's a good point," Colette said. "I agree with Willy. How many times do we look at clouds and see images of faces or animals? Those images are naturally formed by wind blowing the clouds around, not by some alien."

"I don't know..." Drew said. "I'm with Sarah. I think she's right about the evenness of the face. Look at the eye sockets—they're the same size, plus the right side of the face matches the left."

"Hey, class," Dr. Parker interrupted, scanning his wristwatch, "no one knows for sure! It's a mystery, one that I'll leave up to you to solve. Unfortunately, I have to go and talk to another tour group. I hope you all enjoy your visit to the Lowell Observatory."

After Dr. Parker left the theater, Ms. Bogus asked, "Any more questions? I know that one of you has a question in your incredible, supercomputer brain."

"I do," Willy said. "Are there any donuts in that box?" Willy pointed at the box on the table, as the class giggled.

"We'll get to that, Willy," Ms. Bogus said. "Questions?" she persisted.

Willy raised his hand again. "Wouldn't it be awesome to take a trip to Mars?" he asked. "Maybe we could explore the Face on Mars. That would be Mars-velous!"

"I'm game," Drew said. "We could check out that giant volcano that's three times the size of Mt. Everest and maybe roast some 'mars-mallows' over it."

"Just think," Skylar said, "if we could go there, we would make all the other classes green with Martian envy."

"Is it even possible to do that?" Lucia asked.

"Sure!" Colette said, louder than usual. "If we can travel to the moon, we can travel to Mars. It would depend on how close Mars is to us right now."

"Actually," Sarah spoke up, "I read that Mars is going to be at its closest point to us, for the year, this week. But if we use the light bridge, Mars' distance from us is unimportant."

"A light bridge? What's that?" Lucia asked, looking at Ms. Bogus.

"Well, my dear children," she replied, "a light bridge is an accelerated time portal, or doorway—in this case—to Mars, which would reduce the travel time to Mars to just under an hour, instead of six months."

Ms. Bogus gazed at all the expectant faces. "So, do you want to go to Mars?"

Everyone nodded.

"Okay!" Ms. Bogus exclaimed. She opened the brown box, reached in, and pulled out a handful of self-adhesive patches. "Lucia, give one of these to each member of the class," she instructed.

"Just peel off the paper backing," Ms. Bogus said, demonstrating how to put the patch on, "and stick it on your left shoulder."

"These are awesome, Ms. B!" Willy shouted. The patch featured the Jolly Jet the class had used to travel to the Eight Wonders of the World and the words, *Alpine McAlpine School, Trip to Mars* around the edge. The Jolly Jet looked a little different this time—it looked like a rocket ship!

"Okay," Ms. Bogus said, "quiet down, lay your heads back, relax, and listen."

The kids wiggled in their seats to get comfortable. Soon, their eyes closed and their breathing slowed.

Ms. Bogus' melodic voice filled their ears. "The first thing we'll do," she explained, "is escape the earth's gravity to get into orbit. Being in orbit allows us to use Earth's centrifugal force to fling us out into space toward Mars."

CHAPTER FOUR:

Free as a Bird

Willy's eyelids flickered. Ms. B's voice sounded farther away than a minute ago. He opened his eyes and found he was sitting in a window seat on the Jolly Rocket.

He peered out the window to see the ground below, but could barely make out the usual quiltwork pattern of farmland. Only a few puffs of clouds sped past them below, as the curvature of the horizon grew more distinct in the distance. He had never gone this high in a plane before.

Willy suddenly noticed the other children chattering all at once to Ms. B.

"Calm down, everyone," Ms. Bogus said. "The solid rocket boosters should be igniting any second now. Make sure your luggage is stowed in the overhead compartments, your seatbelts are fastened, and your tray tables are in their upright and stowed position." She then scurried down the aisle to check the seatbelts.

She stopped at Colette's chair, which was locked to the floor of the cabin with special wheelchair locks.

"Oh, my!" Ms. Bogus exclaimed, gazing down at Colette's lap. "You don't have a seatbelt. That just won't work. When those rockets ignite, the force will throw you out of your chair and around the cabin."

"I'll take care of her Ms. B," Skylar said, whipping his belt out of the loops on his jeans. "We can fasten her in with this." He quickly weaved the belt around the wheelchair's narrow frame and Colette's **diminutive** waist. He pulled it tight, and buckled it.

Just as Skylar sat and snapped his seatbelt, the boosters ignited, knocking him backward as if a boxer had punched him.

The force pressed all of them back into their seats. The loose skin on their faces contorted, giving them grotesque smiles and thin, backward-shaped eyes. Willy strained against the force. Rotating his head toward the window, he gawked at the changing image, as a deep black ocean of brilliant stars engulfed the bright blue atmosphere of Earth.

Slowly, the pressure on their bodies diminished, releasing their faces from the invisible, viselike grip. Their hair floated freely around them, as did their arms and legs, which they had to consciously hold in place.

A red light flashed on the instrument panel next to Ms. Bogus. "You can remove your seatbelts and move freely about the cabin," she advised, "but be careful, because you are now weightless."

Willy was the first one out of his seat. He pushed off and sailed through the cabin over everyone's head. "This is awesome!" he shouted.

Colette was next. She hovered above her wheelchair for only a second, then pushed off with her arms to soar right behind Willy. Her long, red hair floated behind her as she skimmed freely through the cabin. She had never felt such freedom before! Tears of joy flooded down her cheeks.

Everyone in the Jolly Rocket, including Ms. B, zoomed up and down the cabin, twirling, twisting, flipping, spinning, whirling, looping, and snaking their way over and under everything. It was like watching a pool of fish gone berserk!

"Guys! Guys!" Lucia shouted, holding the armrest of her seat. "It's...it's incredible! It's awesome! It's...it's contagious!"

"Whoa!" Drew said. "You're right. It *is* contagious!"

As the Jolly Rocket passed over the southern tip of Florida, Skylar looked for his twin brother among the flying bodies. "Drew," he called, "I can see where Grams and Papa live. I wish we had a camera."

Sarah wasn't looking at the Earth. She was on the other side of the cabin staring out into space, trying to find one of the many light bridges that could take her to faraway planets. She yearned to explore the unknown.

"Wow!" Willy said. "I think these taste even better in space." Everyone turned to see him surrounded by an open bag of cheese puffs. He intercepted one in his mouth as it floated by him. "Docking maneuver successful," he said, scooping up another weightless puff with his tongue.

The rest of the class joined him in a competition to see who could dock with the most cheese puffs. Giggling uncontrollably, they pushed and shoved to gobble up as many of the crunchy snacks as they could.

Ms. Bogus enjoyed watching the children have fun, but she knew they didn't have time to waste.

"Okay, children," she ordered, "gather around. "We have a lot to cover before we leave orbit and enter the light bridge." She tried to push down her skirt, which now seemed to have a mind of its own. "That's where our trip becomes very interesting."

CHAPTER FIVE:

The Light Bridge

"Who can tell me what centrifugal force is?" Ms. Bogus asked.

Sarah's hand leaped into the air, almost causing her to spin. "I can," she said.

"Okay, Sarah," Ms. Bogus said. "What is centrifugal force, and for a bonus point, tell me how it will help us get to Mars."

Sarah tried to stop wobbling. "Centrifugal force is an outward force that's created when an object rotates around something," she explained. "It's like when you're in a car and you go around a curve in the road without slowing down. The car goes faster due to the rotation around the curve, but the friction of the tires keeps the car on the road. But, any loose objects inside the car are flung outward in a straight line because there's no friction or inward pull holding them in place."

Ms. Bogus nodded in agreement.

"That's what we'll do to propel the Jolly Rocket out into space," Sarah continued. "It's like the rocket is on the end of a string being swung in a circle. Release the string and she'll escape the pull of earth's gravity, which will fling us on a straight line toward the light bridge."

"Very good, Sarah!" Ms. Bogus said, as she glanced at the bank of instruments next to her. "We have exactly six minutes before that happens. Once we're out of Earth's orbit, we'll arrive at the light bridge in just a matter of minutes."

"Ms. B," Willy said, "what is the bridge, exactly?"

"Simply put," Ms. Bogus replied, "this light bridge is only one of many tunnels, or shortcuts, through the space-time continuum. What's that, you ask? It's the where and when of any event. Albert Einstein brought all the thoughts on space and time together with his Special Theory of Relativity.

"It's hard to understand," she continued, "but the mass of large objects in space, like planets or stars, cause space to bend and fold over on itself, creating bridges or shortcuts to different parts of the universe."

The **FASTEN YOUR SEATBELT** sign suddenly lit up, glowing a bright green above Ms. Bogus' head.

Nobody noticed it!

CHAPTER SIX

Yeti, SETI, Schmeti!

"Okay," Willy said, totally confused. "Maybe I'll just hold onto that question until I get to tenth grade science."

"I still want to know if we're going to find any aliens when we get to Mars," Skylar said.

Sarah spun over on her back to face Skylar. "The SETI program has been looking for aliens for decades and hasn't found any."

"What the heck is a SETI?" Drew asked.

"Yeah!" Skylar said. "It sounds like it's the Abominable Snowman."

"That's a yeti," Sarah explained. "SETI stands for the 'Search for Extraterrestrial Intelligence.'"

"I thought the Abominable Snowman was Sasquatch," Drew said.

"That's what it's called in North America," Lucia said. "The yeti lives in the Himalaya Mountains."

"Yeti, SETI, schmeti!" Willy said. "You guys are really confusing me."

"Ms. B," Colette asked, "what's the purpose of this SETI thing?"

"Well, dear," Ms. Bogus said, "some scientists want to try to communicate with other intelligent life in the universe, if there is any. One way to do that is to use large telescopes equipped to listen for radio signals traveling through space."

Ms. Bogus pushed down on her dress, which kept trying to fly upward. "During the last decade," she added, "scientific advances have allowed them to use telescopes equipped with special light sensors to look for very short pulses of laser light that may contain messages."

BRRRRIIIINNNGGG!

Suddenly, a shrill alarm sounded. Instinctively, everyone threw their hands over their ears.

Ms. Bogus glanced up at the seatbelt sign. "Oh, no!" she shouted. "Get your seatbelts on!"

The kids launched themselves off stationary objects and floated toward their seats like Olympic swimmers pushing off the pool wall.

Drew helped Colette into her seat and buckled Skylar's belt around her. He heard the directional rockets fire, knocking the Jolly Rocket out of orbit and flinging it out of the Earth's gravity.

Drew wrapped his arm around a metal post on the back of Colette's chair just as the forward thrust kicked in. The force knocked Ms. Bogus toward the back of the cabin. As she flew past Drew, he snatched her hand and hung on tight.

Drew swung Ms. B into the seat behind Colette, where she quickly buckled her seatbelt. He was about to climb into the seat across the aisle when a bright light radiated through the windows into the Jolly Rocket's cabin. The children were surrounded by the brilliant glow of free radical ions.

"Oh, my gosh!" Ms. Bogus shouted. "The event horizon!"

CHAPTER SEVEN

No Peeking

"We're about to enter the light bridge," Ms. Bogus said. "Close your eyes and keep them closed. No peeking, no matter what! Drew, the blue switch on the instrument panel darkens the windows. Can you get to it?"

"I think so!" Drew shouted. He felt his way along each seat's armrest, with his eyes closed and his legs streaming in the air behind him. Finally, his fingers brushed the bulkhead wall that separated the cabin from the galley. He almost opened his eyes to look for the blue switch, but remembered Ms. B had said to keep them closed—no matter what!

"Ms. B," Drew shouted, "I'm at the instrument panel, but I can't open my eyes to see the switch. What should I do?"

"What was I thinking?" Ms. Bogus said to herself. "It's the..." She pictured the instrument panel in her mind and counted the switches. "It's the top row of switches, fourth switch from the outside edge."

Drew gently touched the panel, feeling each switch until he found the right one. He was about to press it when he remembered something his dad had told him and Skylar many times. "Measure twice, cut once." He counted the switches backward. He found he had been on the fifth switch, not the fourth. He counted them again.

"Drew," Ms. Bogus said, "be careful not to press the fifth switch. It fires the forward thrusters, which you DON'T want to do."

"Now she tells me," Drew muttered. He pressed the correct switch and the cabin instantly darkened. He opened his eyes and looked at everyone. They were all lightly sunburned. "It's okay to open your eyes now," Drew said, fastening himself into Ms. B's seat.

"Well," Ms. Bogus said, taking a deep breath. "That was a close one. Now comes the real dicey part of the trip!"

"Why's that?" Lucia asked.

"Remember when I told you that space is bent and folded?" Ms. Bogus said, still trying to smooth out her dress. "Because of the way it's curved, it folds over on itself. It's kind of like taking a sheet of paper and folding it like a Z."

"That's cool," Willy said. "What's wrong with that?"

"Well," Ms. Bogus explained, "the light bridge is a like a straight line that intersects all of the bends of the fold. But because Mars is so close to Earth right now, the bridge loops around the other side of Mars just past the asteroid belt, between Mars and Jupiter, and takes us to the back side of Mars."

"Ms. B," Colette asked, "are you trying to tell us that we have to go through the asteroid belt?"

"Yes, dear," Ms. Bogus said, unconsciously fiddling with the string of pearls around her neck. "The asteroids amble in and out of the light bridge all the time. I'm hoping the navigation computer can spot them fast enough to zig out of their path."

"So, we could be flattened like a—" Willy said before being interrupted by a loud alarm again.

BRRRRIIIINNNGGG!

"Children!" Ms. Bogus shouted. "Hang on tight! This could be a wwilld rriiiddde!" The Jolly Rocket rolled over on its back and swooped downward.

Drew had been staring at the instrument panel next to him. One of the push switches had the word *Monitor* printed on it. He pushed it. Suddenly, a large television monitor swung out of the ceiling at the front of

the cabin. Next to the *Monitor* switch was another one that read *External View*.

When he pushed that one, the screen came to life. The image showed the Jolly Rocket soaring through the middle of a gigantic, bright, triangular crystalline prism. The prism reflected any source of light, which refracted into a beautiful array of colors.

Ms. Bogus and the children were speechless. That was, until a group of asteroids appeared on the screen in front of them.

AAAHHHHH! Everyone screamed!

CHAPTER EIGHT:

Wild Roller Coaster Ride

The Jolly Rocket executed a perfect barrel roll around the first asteroid, dived under the next, squeezed by the third one, and then performed a flawless outside loop over the top of another. She *zoomed*, squeezed, zigged, *zagged*, dove, *rolled*, and *skidded* around the rest of the asteroids.

"Hang on!" Ms. Bogus shouted.

The children's eyes grew wide. The largest asteroid of all was blocking the whole prism. Suddenly, the children were straining against their seatbelts as the Jolly Rocket dove toward the lower right corner of the prism. Just before it would have crashed into the crystalline matrix of the bridge, it straightened out and soared through a little tunnel at the corner of the bridge.

Before the children could blink, they exploded out of the end of the bridge with Mars in front of them and the Earth shining brightly in the distance.

Willy tossed his hands into the air. "Man, that was awesome *and* contagious," he said.

Skylar looked over at Colette. Her knuckles were white from gripping the wheels on either side of her wheelchair. "Are you okay?" he asked.

"Yeah! I am now," Colette said.

"You can relax and let go of your wheels now," Skylar said, brushing his hair out of his eyes. "We've made it in one piece."

"I know," Colette said, slowly relaxing her body. "Is that what it's like on a roller coaster?"

"Kind of," Skylar said. "It's bumpier on a coaster and they're not able to make some of the turns that we just made. Haven't you ever been on a roller coaster ride?"

"No," she said, "my mom never lets me go. I think she's afraid I'll panic."

"How did you like it?" Skylar asked.

"It might take some getting used to, but I think I could learn to love it," Colette replied with a big smile.

Ms. Bogus could feel the forward thrusters firing to bring them into orbit around Mars. Her dress wanted to float upward off her lap again. Next time I'm wearing pants, she thought. However, that thought quickly left her mind when she felt and heard a loud **RRRRUMBLE!**

CHAPTER NINE:

In a Jam

"Ms. B," Lucia shouted "what's that?"

"It's okay, dear," Ms. Bogus said, figuring out what was happening. "That's just the Jolly Rocket entering the outer layer of Mars' atmosphere. Does anyone remember what the atmosphere of Mars is made of?"

"That's easy," Sarah said. "It's made up mostly of carbon dioxide, with small amounts of nitrogen, argon, and a tiny bit of oxygen."

"Very good, Sarah," Ms. Bogus said. "And how does that compare to our own atmosphere back on Earth?"

Ms. Bogus saw Sarah's hand fly into the air again. "Does anyone else, besides Sarah, know the answer?"

As Colette spoke up, Sarah put her hand down. "Yes, Ms. B," she replied. "It's about three-quarters nitrogen, less than a quarter oxygen, and just tiny amounts of carbon dioxide and argon."

"That's right, Colette," Ms Bogus said, just as the red *Descend* light flashed on her instrument panel. She pressed the blue switch to lighten the windows. "Okay, children! It's time for us to descend to the planet's surface, so keep your eye out for the surface features we talked about earlier today."

"Wow!" Skylar said. "It really is a red planet. Nothing but red!"

"Everything looks so barren, Ms. B," Colette commented.

"Yeah," Drew added, "it kind of reminds me of the Australian Outback that I visited last summer."

"Look at that!" Willy shouted, pointing out the window to the north polar ice cap. "Now, that would be some fun sledding!"

"Scientists believe," Ms. Bogus explained, "that the northern ice cap is made of frozen water, not frozen carbon dioxide, like the southern ice cap."

"That's awesome, Ms. B," Lucia said, "but can we go there?"

"Yes, dear," Ms. Bogus said. "Let me just advise the autopilot where to take us." She pressed a green button on the instrument panel, and a laptop computer dropped out of the panel in front of her.

Ms. Bogus' fingers flew over the keyboard. She pressed *Enter*. Nothing happened.

"Ms. B," Skylar observed, "it doesn't look like we're descending anymore."

"Yeah!" Willy said. "It's like we hit an invisible ceiling and we can't get through it."

Ms. Bogus tried again, but got the same result. Nothing! Suddenly, a flashing message in big red letters appeared across the screen:

VERTICAL GYRO ACCELEROMETER
JAMMED!

BACKUP VERTICAL GYRO
ACCELEROMETER FAILED
SNYC TEST!

CHAPTER TEN:

Teamwork

"Oh, my!" Ms. Bogus exclaimed.

"What's wrong now, Ms. B?" Willy asked.

"We can't descend or ascend because our vertical gyro isn't working," Ms. Bogus replied with a worried look.

"Don't they put more than one of those on an aircraft like this?" Drew asked.

"Yes," Ms. Bogus said, "but our backup failed something called a Sync Test. I think that means it failed to hook up to the Jolly Rocket's engine thrust computers."

"What does that all mean, Ms. B?" Colette asked.

"It means we can't go down to the surface or back up into space," Ms. Bogus answered.

"You mean we're just going to keep flying around the planet until we run out of fuel?" Willy asked.

"That's correct," Ms. Bogus said, "but only if we don't find a solution to the problem. Remember, children, there is always a way to **resolve** any situation. You just need to think about it and figure out the best course of action to take."

"First, I think we need to find out where the vertical thing-a-ma-gig is," Drew suggested. "Maybe we can fix it. My dad says that 90 percent of the time it's usually something simple causing a problem."

"Okay," Ms. Bogus said, as her fingers flew over the keyboard. Several images flashed across the screen until it froze on one. "According to this," she said, "the main vertical gyro is in an electronics compartment below the cockpit, but the backup is in a smaller compartment behind the back galley."

The kids quickly unbuckled their seatbelts, and bounded back toward the galley.

"If it's behind the galley," Sarah said, "maybe we have to move those little carts that hold all the food."

"Food!" Willy said, peeking over the rest of the group. "Did I hear someone say 'food?'"

"Willy," Ms. Bogus said, "we'll have something to eat after we solve this problem."

Drew and Skylar yanked the carts out of the way. "There it is!" Skylar cried. "Good call, Sarah."

Drew unlocked the access door and pulled it open. He stuck his head inside the opening and looked around.

"I found it!" he shouted, as he tried to wiggle through the hole. "But I can't fit. The hole's too small."

"No, it's not," Willy said. "Now I'll show you why it's good to be skinny." But Willy couldn't fit through, either. One after another, the children each tried to get through the opening, but no one could fit.

"What are we going to do now?" Willy asked.

Colette wiggled her way to the front of the group. "Let me try," she said. "I'm smaller than all of you."

"Are you sure you want to do this?" Ms. Bogus asked.

"We're a team," Colette said, "and every member of a team has to do what they can to help. I know I can do this."

Colette used her arms to push through the opening. "Okay," she said, "I'm in. These boxes all look the same. Oh! Here's the one marked *V. Gyro Accel.* It's way in the back. I can..."

Colette stopped talking. Ms. Bogus looked worried.

Several long seconds passed. "I feel it!" Willy cried. "We're going down again!"

The class started to cheer, as Colette stuck her head through the hole.

"Mission accomplished!" Colette shouted, louder than she had ever said anything before. "There was a round metal plug that wasn't tightened, so I tightened it!"

Lucia wrapped her in a big bear hug. "That was great!" she cried.

CHAPTER ELEVEN:

Murphy's Law

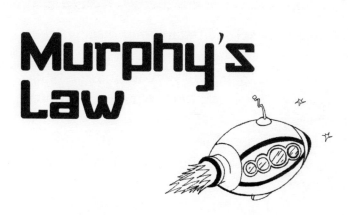

The approach to the northern polar ice cap was picture-perfect.

"Class," Ms. Bogus said, "if you reach under your seats you will find a helmet with a headlight and an Oxygen Ion Force Field Generator. Once we leave this ship, you cannot remove the helmet. The front clear shield is made of the same material as the Jolly Rocket's windows, except it will automatically adjust from light to dark."

"Now," Ms. Bogus instructed, "remove the generator from its pouch and slide the clip onto your belt or the waistband of your pants." Ms. Bogus pushed several buttons on the instrument panel and the monitor disappeared back into the ceiling.

"These generators create a force field of positive ions around your body, while converting the planet's carbon dioxide into breathable oxygen," Ms. Bogus said.

"Does the force field protect us if we fall or scrape against a rock?" Sarah asked.

"Oh, no, dear," Ms. Bogus said. "It's not that kind of force field. It's like an invisible spacesuit. It only protects our bodies from the harsh atmosphere of Mars by creating an environment where our bodies can survive."

Willy held his generator in his hands. He turned it on and off. He felt a rush of coolness from head to toe, and the air around him tasted fresh. "How long will it work?" he asked.

"If you look on the front, you will see a battery strength indicator," Ms. Bogus said. "The generator's battery charge only lasts about two hours. Naturally, some generators will last longer than others. But don't worry, we'll be back with plenty of time to spare."

Colette turned to Lucia and whispered, "I hate it when people say we shouldn't worry, because that's when you really need to start worrying, because something always goes wrong. It's Murphy's Law."

"Murphy's Law? What's that?" Lucia whispered back.

"Murphy's Law states that whatever can go wrong, will go wrong," Colette replied. "It's kind of like hanging around with Willy. You know that at some point, he's going to run full speed into something without thinking about it, causing all of us a problem."

Sarah leaned across the aisle. "The full Murphy's Law says, 'whatever can go wrong, will go wrong at the most inappropriate time,'" she explained. "So we'd better stay nice and close to each other."

CHAPTER TWELVE:

A Sledding We Will Go

The children grabbed a couple of large serving trays that were perfect to use as sleds. Willy was the first one out of the Jolly Rocket. He slid wildly around on the icy snow as he weaved his way over to the closest hill. It wasn't too steep and the snow was packed just right.

"*YAHOOOOOO!*" Willy shouted, as he ran and threw himself down on the tray. Using his feet to steer, he slipped around mounds of snow and raced downhill. He valiantly tried to keep his bright red scarf from whipping around his face as the sled picked up speed. He expected to come to a slow stop at the bottom, but instead, he kept going, and going, and going! He suddenly realized that because the gravity was less on Mars than on Earth, he would probably slide for miles without stopping.

Willy dug his feet into the snow and came to a quick stop at the top of what appeared to be another hill. When he stood up, he saw that it was actually the edge of an ice cliff, with a vertical drop of several hundred feet.

"Whew!" Willy huffed and puffed, out of breath after his wild ride. "Just in time!"

"Willy!" Drew shouted, "isn't this cool?" Drew and Skylar had pulled up right behind him. He saw Lucia and Sarah approaching them fast.

"Stop!" he shouted, waving at the two girls. Both girls dug their feet into the snow and careened to a stop.

Lucia could see the concern on his face. "What's wrong?" she asked.

Willy was watching Colette come down the hill. She couldn't use her feet to stop herself. "Colette can't stop!" he shouted, as he ran toward her. "She's going to go over the edge of the cliff!"

As Colette started to pass Willy, he dove on top of her. He quickly dug the toes of his shoes into the snow, but his extra weight made them slide further. Willy wrapped his arms around her shoulders and rolled off the slick tray onto his back. *POOF!* They sank into a fluffy snowdrift, just a few feet from the edge of the cliff.

"That was contagious!" Colette said. She had no idea she was so close to danger.

Willy laid his head back in the snow. "Yeah! Contagious!"

"Hey, guys," Drew said, "I think we should find a safer hill to go down. Don't you, Willy?

Willy raised his head and gave Drew a thumbs-up.

CHAPTER THIRTEEN:

Please Don't Erupt!

Once the children returned from sledding and removed their Oxygen Ion Force Field Generators, the Jolly Rocket was off again, traveling briskly over the surface of Mars.

"Where are we going now, Ms. B?" Skylar asked, as he felt the Jolly Rocket slowing down.

"Look out the window, Skylar," Willy said, before Ms. B could answer.

The class gazed out the windows at Olympus Mons, and were amazed that the volcano was so large they couldn't even see the other end of its lava bed. Parts of it looked like a blackish-red lake where the once-molten lava had hardened into smooth, black rock.

"Olympus Mons," Ms. Bogus explained, "is the largest volcano known in our solar system. It protrudes almost 17 miles above the surrounding plains, which makes it three times taller than Mt. Everest. It's also 342 miles across, making it about the size of the state of Arizona."

"Look at those lava formations over there," Willy pointed out the window. "One of them looks like a matador and a bull. I also see a face of a dog. Hey, those are some examples of rock formations looking like familiar things. It happens on Earth and I believe the same thing is happening here with the Face on Mars!"

"That lava bed reminds me of a frozen lake in the winter," Drew said, munching on a bag of potato chips. "There are probably just a few inches of hardened lava rock, and then below that is the smoldering, bubbly, hot lava stuff."

"Drew," Skylar asked, "how can it be like a frozen lake, when a lake is cold, not hot?"

"I know that," Drew said. "I mean that they're similar in the way that they both appear harmless and pretty. But beneath the calm exterior lies certain death, whether it's molten lava or freezing water!"

"Is that true, Ms. B?" Lucia asked.

"Drew may be right," Ms. Bogus said. "Some scientists believe that Olympus Mons may still have some life in her. Several of them believe it might not take much to cause her to wake up and erupt again."

"Oh!" Lucia said. "Please don't erupt today!"

"Hey," Willy said, still staring at the miles of hard lava just below them. "Is it okay if that lava bed is cracking as we fly over it?"

Ms. Bogus leaped to the window. "Oh, no! Seatbelts!" she yelled, jumping back to the computer. She frantically typed in new commands. The Jolly Rocket surged skyward, away from the volcano.

"Look at that!" Willy screamed. With their faces glued to the windows, the kids watched a bright-red lava plume explode into the Martian sky. The Jolly Rocket seemed to kick into a higher gear and sped even faster away from the bulging volcano.

"Did we cause that?" Sarah squawked.

"You're the smart one," Drew said. "You tell us!"

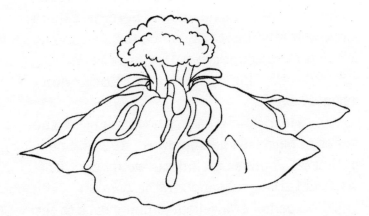

CHAPTER FOURTEEN:

Pull up! Pull up!

The Jolly Rocket raced across the smoke-filled, crimson sky as geysers of glowing red lava continued to erupt below it. Finally, the children and Ms. Bogus let out a big sigh of relief. The Jolly Rocket had escaped safely.

Ms. Bogus turned the Jolly Rocket toward their next destination. The children gathered at the windows again to watch the lava light show behind them.

"That's contagious!" Willy said. "I'll bet the heat from the Jolly Rocket's engines caused the hard lava bed to crack, releasing all that stuff pent-up inside the volcano."

"Stop being so dramatic, Willy," Sarah said. "There are probably a million reasons why it erupted right now."

"Okay, everyone," Ms. Bogus said, "gather around. We have just enough time to go to the *Valles Marineris*."

"What's that?" Lucia asked.

"It's Latin for *Mariner Valleys*," Ms. Bogus explained. "It was named after the *Mariner 9* spacecraft, which orbited Mars in 1971. It's the largest known canyon in our solar system. It's way, way, longer than our own Grand Canyon. In fact, the *Valles Marineris* stretches over one-fourth of Mars' surface, which is the distance from Los Angeles to Chicago. Plus, it's as wide as the state of Colorado and is also six times deeper than the Grand Canyon."

"Good grief, that's big!" Skylar exclaimed. "Can we go hiking in there?"

"Not if you want to make it to the Face on Mars before we have to head home," Ms. Bogus said. "We don't want to miss the light bridge before it closes up. Otherwise, it will take us six months to get back to Earth!"

She looked out the window. "There's the *Valles Marineris* now! Fasten your seatbelts because we're going in for a closer look."

The large monitor swung out of the ceiling again, showing a magnificent view of the canyon below them. Almost instantly, the Jolly Rocket dove recklessly toward the canyon floor six miles below.

"*WOOO HOOOOOOO!*" The boys waved their arms wildly in the air. "This is the best roller coaster I've ever been on!" screamed Willy.

"*AAAAHHHHHHHH!*" The girls and Ms. Bogus screeched, covering their eyes.

The bottom of the canyon floor grew bigger and closer on the monitor as every second ticked by.

"You're crazy! We're all going to die!" Lucia screamed.

"No, we won't!" Drew shouted. "We'll pull up any second now."

But the Jolly Rocket didn't pull up. If anything, its speed seemed to increase.

"*Pull up!   Pull up!*" Drew shouted, as the kids joined him in the frantic chant.

"*Pull up! Pull up!*"

Ms. Bogus was frozen with fright in her seat, overwhelmed by the thought of the certain death she envisioned on the monitor in front of her.

CHAPTER FIFTEEN:

Rock and Roll

Suddenly, the Jolly Rocket pulled out of its dive, forcing everyone downward into their seats. It settled at an altitude of 500 feet above the canyon floor. The Rocket darted through the canyon, weaving between rock outcroppings, soaring over peaks, and careening around sharp turns.

"*WOOO HOOOOOOO!*" Willy kept shouting. "I love this, Ms. B!"

"That's because you're insane," Colette said.

"You can call me insane, you can call me crazy, but just don't call me boring!" Willy shouted.

"This is just like one of my video games back home," Drew said. "I could do this for hours."

"How fast are we going, Ms. B?" Lucia asked.

Ms. Bogus fingered her pearls with one hand as her other hand pressed another button on the instrument panel. Flight information popped up on the monitor, showing direction, airspeed, and altitude. The airspeed reading hovered around 1700 knots.

"How fast is 1700 knots?" Sarah asked.

"It's about 2,000 miles per hour, dear," Ms. Bogus said, as she typed more commands into the computer. The Jolly Rocket slowed to 200 knots.

"Oh!" Willy cried. "Don't slow down, Ms. B."

"What's that?" Colette shouted.

"What's what?" Lucia asked.

"Something moved over by those rocks," Colette said.

"I thought I saw something move, too," Skylar agreed. "It was just out of the corner of my eye, but I could swear it had a thin body and a big oval shaped head, and it was kind of green."

"Good one, Skylar!" Drew said. "Mom always says you're the creative one. I can't wait to tell her this one."

"No!" Skylar insisted. "Really, I saw something."

"Yeah!" Drew teased. "Me, too. But I thought he looked more like Michael Jordan. If fact, I could have sworn he was making a hook shot to the net."

"Whatever," Skylar shrugged. "You never believe anything I tell you anyway."

The class hadn't noticed it, but the Jolly Rocket was slowly climbing out of the canyon. "Okay, class, I hope you enjoyed that because I definitely didn't," Ms. Bogus said, wrapping some loose strands of her rumpled hair behind her ear.

"Our last stop...is the Face on Mars!" she announced.

CHAPTER SIXTEEN

Turtle Artists

The Jolly Rocket hovered above the Face on Mars for a few seconds before descending slowly to the surface.

"I don't know," Skylar said, looking out the window at the ground below. "If this was built by intelligent life, they better go back to exterior decorating and landscaping school, because it looks just like a rocky butte to me."

"What if it's some type of art?" Lucia asked. "Is it possible that some galactic traveler left his artistic mark on the planet?"

"You mean this could be like when we go camping and scratch our names or initials into a tree?" Colette asked.

"Exactly," Lucia answered.

"But it's ugly!" Skylar said.

"Have you seen what people like to pass off as art?" Willy said. "Some of it looks really weird!"

The Jolly Rocket landed with a jolt.

"Well," Drew said, as he unfastened his seatbelt and stood to stretch. "My bottom hurts from sitting so long. Let's see if this alien space artist is as good as Michelangelo."

"Why would an alien want to be like a Teenage Mutant Ninja Turtle?" Willy asked. "Then again, being an alien, he may already look like one. But I always thought that Leonardo was the better looking of the two. I think it was because his shell was always a little shinier than Raphael's, Donatello's, or even Michelangelo's."

"You're a goofball!" Sarah cried. "Michelangelo is one of the most famous artists of all time!" A barrage of pillows pounded Willy's head.

CHAPTER SEVENTEEN:

Alien Robots

Drew led the way down the ramp at the back of the Jolly Rocket. Stepping onto the surface of Mars felt eerie. He knew that the environment around him was poisonous, but he couldn't feel it. All he felt was coolness surrounding his body, like the feeling when you enter an air-conditioned house after playing outside. He looked down at the battery indicator on his generator. It was full.

Willy stamped his foot on the ground. "Feels like rock to me," he said. "I don't think this is art, either. It's just a butte and not even a nice-looking butte at that."

Colette was the last one down the ramp. She wasn't in her wheelchair anymore. Instead, she sat on something resembling a small jet ski. It produced a cushion of air beneath it, allowing it to fly over the rough terrain.

"Over there!" Lucia shouted. "I saw something move!"

"Oh, boy!" Drew said. "Here we go again."

Lucia began running toward the mysterious object. Colette and Sarah hurried behind her, followed by Skylar, Willy, and Ms. Bogus. Drew stayed behind. He noticed that Ms. Bogus was having trouble keeping up with the kids, so he helped her over the rocky ledges.

"It went in here!" Lucia shouted, as she approached the entrance to a cave. She stopped just outside the cave, not sure if she wanted to go in or not. Her flashlight beam lit up the entrance.

"Are we on a little green men wild goose chase?" Drew asked, after catching up with them.

"No!" Lucia said. "This was something mechanical, like a robot."

"Oh, boy!" Drew exclaimed. "Now, instead of seeing aliens, you're seeing alien robots?" He looked at Skylar.

"Hey," Skylar said, "don't look at me. I didn't see anything this time. But I think this cave ends our little mystery. This isn't art or anything designed by intelligent life. It's just a natural part of the planet."

"Contagious!" Willy said, as he moved to the front of the group. "What are we waiting for? Let's go robot hunting."

Before Ms. Bogus could say anything, he disappeared into the cave.

"Murphy's Law," Colette muttered to herself, as she followed the rest of the children into what she was sure would turn out to be an "inappropriate time."

CHAPTER EIGHTEEN:

So Far From Home

Willy was way ahead of everyone else. "Slow down, Willy," Sarah shouted. "We can't keep up with those long legs of yours."

"Whoa!" Willy yelled. "This is the coolest thing ever!"

"Did you find it?" Lucia shouted.

"I found a robot," Willy said, "but it doesn't look like an alien robot."

Panting, the class caught up to Willy. Their eyes followed his pointing finger. Stuck in a tiny, U-shaped cutout in the cave rock was a small, flat-topped vehicle.

"What's that written on the side of it?" Skylar asked.

Willy took a closer look. "It says, So...jour...ner," Willy said.

"*Sojourner*?" Sarah repeated with amazement. "Ms. Bogus, isn't that the name of the rover NASA sent here on the Mars *Pathfinder* mission?"

"Yes, it is," Ms. Bogus said, standing at the back of the group. "It landed on Mars on July 4, 1997. It was considered a success, because both *Pathfinder* and *Sojourner* lasted much longer than the scientists expected."

"But it's **obsolete** now," Colette said, "because we sent two new rovers here last year."

"The poor thing is so far from home," Lucia said.

Willy kept trying to reach it. "It may be far from home, but I don't think this is what you saw come in here, Lucia," Willy said.

"Why not?" Lucia asked.

Drew and Skylar hoisted Willy up so he could stretch closer to the rover. "Because," he grunted, "this thing looks D-E-A-D, dead."

Ms. Bogus spotted a side tunnel and took a few cautious steps toward it. "Maybe whatever you saw went down this tunnel, dear," she said.

Willy wrapped his hand around the rubber-coated antennae.

Everyone, except Ms. Bogus, moved closer to Willy.

"*AAAAHHHHHHHH!*"

Ms. Bogus whirled around. The children were gone! In their place was a large hole in the cave floor.

"Oh, my! Oh, my!" Ms. Bogus shrieked.

CHAPTER NINETEEN:

Sliding on Sand

Sarah and Lucia held on tightly to the back of Colette's hover chair, as the kids plummeted down a massive landslide of sand.

Willy tucked *Sojourner* under his arm to protect it. Drew and Skylar were tumbling on either side of him, and he could hear the girls screaming behind him. But he couldn't hear Ms. B, like he had on the ride through the canyon. Either she was too scared to scream or she wasn't with them, he thought. He wasn't sure which was worse.

Willy reached down into the sand and felt smooth rock only a few inches below him. This was like a water slide, except he didn't know where or when this slide was going to end. He spun around a corner, dropped vertically, rounded another bend, and then plunged into a huge pile of sand and bodies.

Slowly, the children struggled to their feet. The first thing they all noticed was that Ms. B wasn't there.

"Can you guys give me a hand?" Colette asked. She had been knocked off the hover scooter, which was stuck awkwardly in the sand.

Drew and Willy wrestled the scooter out of its sandy grip. As soon as they let go of it, the scooter spun itself back upright and hovered just inches above the cave floor.

Drew lifted Colette onto the scooter. "Thanks, guys. How far do you think we fell?" she asked, smiling.

"Why are you smiling?" Lucia asked.

"Uh, well," Colette said. "I hate to say it, but that was contagious! I am having so much fun on this trip doing things I've never tried to do before and working with all of you as a team!"

"But, we're in a cave," Lucia interrupted, "underground, on a planet far from home, with these force field thingy's that are going to run out of battery juice, and in case you haven't noticed, it's dark down here, and Ms. B is gone, and we have no idea how to get out of here!" Lucia was becoming frantic.

Colette moved closer to Lucia and pulled her into a hug. "You're right, Lucia, but look at what we've accomplished together. Skylar helped fasten me into my seat at the beginning of our journey. He didn't have to risk his life for me. Then, Drew saved me, and Ms. B, and kept us all from going blind. It's been quite a trip!"

"And you fixed that gyro thingy," Willy said.

"After Sarah figured out where to look for it," Colette added.

"And we made it out of the path of the volcano's lava and survived that wild and crazy ride through the canyon," Skylar said.

"Yeah," Drew said, "we all need to remember what Ms. B told us. 'There is always a way to **resolve** any situation we find ourselves in.'"

"Drew's right!" Willy said. "We just need to stay calm and think our way through this, which brings us back to Colette's question of how far we slid before ending up here."

"I counted the time," Sarah said. "It took us about 14 seconds to slide down the hill. So, doing the math in my head, I think we slid somewhere around 110 feet—give or take a few feet."

Skylar spit on his finger and stuck it into the air. "Hey," he said, "I feel a breeze. It's blowing that way." He pointed beyond a narrow opening between the cave wall and the huge pile of sand.

Willy, as usual, was the first to squeeze through the opening. He still had *Sojourner* tucked under his arm. "I guess we've definitely proved that the face above us is not an intergalactic piece of art or some ancient, secret, alien military outpost or—"

Willy froze.

CHAPTER TWENTY:

Eenie, Meenie, Minie, Moe

As each of Willy's classmates streamed through the hole and scrambled to his side, they stopped and stared at the oddity in front of them.

They found themselves in a large cavern where the ceiling was at least 60 feet above their heads. Three perfectly round and evenly spaced tunnels were cut into the cave wall at the far end of the cavern.

"They're just tunnels," Skylar said.

"Yeah," Sarah replied, "but have you ever seen natural tunnels that were perfectly round like those?"

"They had to be cut by some sort of machinery," Lucia suggested.

"I don't think so," Colette said. "The lava tubes in Hawaii are nice and round like these, so it's possible that these were made naturally."

"So which one of those tunnels is our best choice to get out of here?" Skylar asked.

The kids stared at each other in silence.

"ET, must phone home," Willy muttered. He took a marker out of his pocket and printed some letters on the back of *Sojourner*.

"I have an idea!" he said. "Everyone shine your helmet lights on *Sojourner's* solar panels. If we can get it to power up, its internal mapping system may be able to find a way out through one of those tunnels."

"Great idea!" Sarah cried. "Let's do it!"

The children aimed their helmet lights at *Sojourner's* panels. One minute passed, then two minutes, then three.

"I don't think this is working," Drew said. "Why don't we just try 'eenie, meenie, minie, moe' to get out of here."

"Let's keep doing it for another minute," Willy said. "Its batteries have been dead for so long that maybe it has to charge up a little before it comes back to life."

They waited another minute. "I hate to say it," Skylar said, "but I think Drew is right."

BEEP, BEEP, BEEP! Sojourner suddenly shuddered.

"It's working!" Lucia screamed. "I can't believe it! It's actually working!"

Sojourner moved forward an inch and stopped.

"I don't know," Drew said. "I think it died again."

"Maybe we should just take a vote on which tunnel to try and go for it," Sarah said. "We may get lucky, but then again, maybe none of them lead out of here."

BEEP, BEEP, BEEP! Sojourner sounded again, as it began shuffling across the cavern floor. When it neared the tunnels, it hesitated for just a second, and then scooted into the tunnel on the right.

"That's the tunnel I was going to guess," Skylar said.

"Yeah, right!" Drew said.

"I was, really!" Skylar exclaimed.

"You guys can argue later," Colette said. "Let's just focus on where this machine is leading us."

PING, PING, PING.

"Did that come from *Sojourner?*" Drew asked.

"No!" Lucia cried. "It came from my Oxygen Ion Force Field Generator. I only have 15 minutes of battery life left!"

"We've got to hurry," Skylar urged.

"Hold it!" Sarah said. "I have an idea. Everybody hold hands—now!"

The kids immediately linked hands. As they followed *Sojourner* down the dark tunnel, Willy's helmet light died.

CHAPTER TWENTY-ONE

In the Dark!

"Oh boy!" Willy said. "It's a good thing I eat my carrots so I can see in the dark."

"Lucia, what does your battery indicator show now?" Sarah asked.

"It's gone back up into the green again," Lucia said. "It must be taking juice from all of your generators."

"That's what I was hoping for," Sarah said. Her smile turned to a **grimace** when her own helmet light flickered, then turned to black.

"We can't lose more light!" Drew exclaimed. "Everyone who has a light, make sure you're shining it on *Sojourner*'s panels."

Lucia let go of everyone's hands and grabbed the bottom hem of her knit sweater. She yanked on a piece of yarn and the sweater began to unravel. After pulling out about 20 feet of yarn, she tied a slipknot in one end.

Skylar's light went out.

Lucia hurried forward so she was right behind *Sojourner*. A second before her helmet light died, she threw the slipknot over the tallest of *Sojourner*'s several antennas.

"Willy," she ordered, "take my hand! Everyone else, grab each other's hands again."

Drew's light went out.

"I hope none of you are afraid of the boogey man, because I think he's about to pay us a visit," Willy said, a tremble in his usually jovial voice.

Colette's light blinked twice and went dead, plunging them into darkness.

Lucia spoke up. "Just walk in a single file line and no matter what, don't let go of anyone's hand, because in this darkness you may never find it again," she said. Her voice was firm. She led the group further through the darkness with each little tug of the yarn tied to *Sojourner*.

PING, PING, PING, PING.

More generators began to signal their 15-minute warning. No one said a word. They continued to stumble through the darkness.

"Hey," Skylar said. "Is it my imagination, or can I see some light?"

"I see it, too!" Willy cried. "I can see the outline of something."

Lucia saw light ahead, too. "We're almost there!" she shouted. "I can see *Sojourner* ahead of us!"

"Hello!" Ms. B's voice echoed in the tunnel. "Can you hear me?"

"YES! YES! YES!" The children jumped up and down and squeezed each other in huge hugs.

Sojourner led them to the tunnel exit where Ms. B was standing. The girls raced up to her and wrapped their arms around her waist, while Drew, Willy, and Skylar gave each other high-fives.

"How did you know where to find us?" Lucia asked, burying her head into Ms. B's shoulder.

"Your force field generators have a tracking system built into them," Ms. Bogus explained. "I knew where you were, but I wasn't sure how to get to you. However in the world did you find your way out?" she asked.

Willy picked up *Sojourner* to keep it from running off. They all looked at each other.

"Teamwork!" they shouted.

CHAPTER TWENTY-TWO:

Pillow Fight

"Come on Ms. B," Willy said, his hand resting on *Sojourner*, which was fastened into the seat next to him. "Do we have to go? I was hoping we'd get a chance to go back to Olympus Mons to see if it's still erupting."

The Jolly Rocket broke orbit around Mars and flung itself toward the crystalline light bridge as it headed back to earth.

"I'm sorry, Willy," Ms. Bogus said, "but we're barely going to make it to the light bridge in time, as it is."

The children were scattered around the cabin, chattering about their Mars adventure.

"*Owwww!*" Something smacked Skylar in the back, sending him barreling down the cabin. He spun around to see his brother with a small pillow in his grip.

"So that's how it is, huh," Skylar said, smiling, as he clutched a seatback to stop his weightless flight. He reached into an overhead bin, grabbed a pillow for himself, and tumbled back toward Drew.

Within seconds all the children were swinging pillows wildly at each other, bouncing off the walls, ceiling, floors, seats, and anything else they could use to rebound back into the fray.

Ms. Bogus had hurried up to the galley to escape the pillow war. She knew the children needed to release some of the pent-up energy and anxiety they stored up while in the cave.

"I got you!" Sarah shouted.

"You're mine, Willy!" Drew blared.

"Catch me if you can!" Colette screamed, whirling away from Lucia.

"Drew, you're mine!" shouted Skylar.

As Ms. Bogus watched them, she was reminded of bumper pool. Lucia whacked Willy, who flew backward into Colette, who plowed into Sarah, who slammed into Skylar, who crashed into Drew, who ricocheted off the ceiling into Willy.

RRRRIIIINNNNGGGG!

The alarm sounded again, warning them they would soon enter the light bridge. Ms. Bogus didn't have to tell the children that playtime was over. They hurried back to their seats and fastened their seatbelts.

"I know you children have got to be tired," Ms. Bogus said. "Put your heads back, relax, and close your eyes. And Willy," Ms. Bogus added, "if you want, you can use your imagination to take us back to Olympus Mons."

Epilogue

"But I don't want to imagine it," Willy said, opening his eyes. "I want to really go there..." He looked around, and saw they were already back in the space theater. He saw *Sojourner* sitting on a table in the corner.

"I don't think we really went to Mars," Skylar said. "It all happened too fast."

"Then how do you explain that we all have the same memories?" Lucia asked.

"Yeah," Colette agreed. "I remember the exact feeling of being free from this chair and floating weightless around the cabin. And

I've never seen darkness like we did in the cave when our lights went out."

Willy jumped in. "It was real," he said, pointing to *Sojourner*. "Otherwise, that wouldn't be here with us. Plus, we all know now that the Face on Mars is naturally made."

"I still don't agree with that," Sarah said, stubbornly crossing her arms across her chest. "The fact that those tunnels were so perfect speaks of intelligent design, not something natural. That whole face could have been designed."

"We may never know whether the face was formed naturally or by intelligent beings," Colette said, "or whether our trip was real or not. But I do know that when we work together, we can accomplish great things!"

As they were leaving the theater, Willy and Drew passed *Sojourner*.

"Drew, I can prove we really went to Mars," Willy said.

"Oh yeah?" Drew said. "How?"

"Do you remember when I wrote something on *Sojourner* in the cavern?" Willy asked.

"Yes," Drew said. "I remember that. What did you write?"

"I wrote my initials, RW, which stand for Robert Williams," Willy said, as he turned *Sojourner* around to face Drew. "What does it say?" he asked.

"Well, I'll be," Drew said. "It says RW. We really did go to Mars!"

"See!" Willy said. "I told you!"

The End

ABOUT THE AUTHOR

Carole Marsh is an author and publisher who has written many works of fiction and non-fiction for young readers. She travels throughout the United States and around the world to research her books. In 1979 Carole Marsh was named Communicator of the Year for her corporate communications work with major national and international corporations.

Marsh is the founder and CEO of Gallopade International, established in 1979. Today, Gallopade International is widely recognized as a leading source of educational materials for every state and many countries. Marsh and Gallopade were recipients of the 2004 Teachers' Choice Award. Marsh has written more than 50 Carole Marsh Mysteries™. In 2007, she was named Georgia Author of the Year. Years ago, her children, Michele and Michael, were the original characters in her mystery books. Today, they continue the Carole Marsh Books tradition by working at Gallopade. By adding grandchildren Grant and Christina as new mystery characters, she has continued the tradition for a third generation.

Ms. Marsh welcomes correspondence from her readers. You can e-mail her at fanclub@gallopade.com, visit carolemarshmysteries.com, or write to her in care of Gallopade International, P.O. Box 2779, Peachtree City, Georgia, 30269 USA.

Book Club
Talk About It!:

1. Who was your favorite character? Why?

2. What is Murphy's Law? Can you apply it to an event that has happened to you recently?

3. Why did Colette cry tears of joy when she first experienced weightlessness?

4. Drew and Skylar's father told them to "measure twice, cut once." What is the meaning of this saying and what is important about it?

5. Do you think there is extraterrestrial life in the universe, or more specifically, on Mars?

6. What was your favorite part of the story? Why?

7. Teamwork is an important theme of the story. Can you remember a time in your own life where teamwork was important to accomplish a task?

8. Throughout the story, Drew continually helps those in need. Why is it important to help people in need or to help those that are less fortunate than you?

9. Willy says, "You can call me insane, you can call me crazy, but just don't call me boring!" What is Willy saying about himself? Do you think this is a good way to live your life?

10. Why do you think our country and other countries send spacecraft to explore other planets?

Book Club
Bring It to Life!

1. Mars Spacecraft! Organize your book club into groups of four. Draw a name of one of the amazing spacecraft that have explored Mars out of a hat. Research the spacecraft that you draw and make a poster board presenting your findings. Make sure to include five facts about your spacecraft, a picture of the spacecraft, and an interesting discovery your spacecraft made.

2. Be a Martian! Use pipe cleaners to create your own special Martian antennae to wear during your time at Book Club. Have fun!

3. Explore Mars! Pretend you are a Mars explorer. Write your own journal entry for a day of exploration on the surface of Mars. Make sure to include important findings, dangers you come across, interesting observations you make, and where you eat and rest during the day. Be creative! Explain how it feels to be on the surface of Mars. Are you scared? Are you excited? Let everyone know!

4. Martian artwork! Draw a picture of what you think Mars would look like if you were riding on the Jolly Rocket in Ms. Bogus' class. Include your own idea of what the Face on Mars may look like, as well as how you picture the surface of Mars. Don't forget to make it red!

GLOSSARY

careen: to lean to one side while in motion

 diminutive: small; tiny

fray: a fight or a battle

generator: a machine that converts one form of energy to another

 grimace: a twisting of the muscles of the face

grotesque: odd or unnatural in shape or color; ugly

hysteria: uncontrollable outburst of emotion or fear

jovial: merry; jolly

 obsolete: no longer in use; out of date

 resolve: to bring to an end; to deal with an issue

ricochet: the motion of an object as it rebounds off a surface

symmetrical: having matching shapes on either side of a center line

Mars Trivia

1. There are 687 Earth days in a Martian year.

2. The Martian volcano *Olympus Mons* is the largest volcano in our solar system. It is about the size of Arizona and is three times taller than Mount Everest.

3. The Martian canyon *Valles Marineris* is the largest canyon in our solar system, stretching the distance from Los Angeles to Chicago. It covers over one fourth of the Martian surface!

4. The Martian atmosphere is made primarily of carbon dioxide—which is toxic in large quantities to life on Earth!

5. Mars has two moons unlike Earth's one moon. Their names are *Phobos* and *Diemos*.

6. The Martian moons are both about 20 kilometers wide.

7. Mars is named after the Roman God of War.

8. Temperatures on the Martian surface are generally very cold. The temperature on Mars ranges from about 220 degrees below zero to 80 degrees Fahrenheit. The average temperature is below zero.

9. Mars is about 137 million miles from the sun.

10. Mars has approximately the same surface area as Earth!

Scavenger Hunt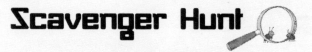

Want to have some fun? Let's go on a scavenger hunt! See if you can find the items below related to the mystery. (Teachers: You have permission to reproduce this page for your students.)

1. ___ A picture of Sojourner, the Mars rover that landed on July 4, 1977 on the Pathfinder mission.

2. ___ A picture of the real Face on Mars.

3. ___ A toy rocket ship

4. ___ A picture of the Lowell Observatory

5. ___ A bag of cheese puffs

6. ___ A flashlight

7. ___ A telescope

8. ___ A toy alien or some sort of alien robot action figure

9. ___ Sunglasses to protect your eyes from solar flares and the event horizon!

10. ___ A red scarf like Billy wore while sledding!

Pop Quiz

1. What danger lies along the Jolly Rocket's path on the light bridge?

2. What do the children do when they get to the northern ice cap?

3. What type of force is required for the Jolly Rocket to leave Earth's gravitational pull and head towards Mars?

4. What number would you divide your Earth weight by to get your Martian weight?

5. What was the name of the observatory the class visited on their field trip?

6. What does the class find in the Face on Mars cave during their final stop on Mars?

7. What game do all the children play (except for Sarah) in the observatory?

8. Who fixes the Jolly Rocket's vertical gyro accelerometer?

Tech Connects

Hey, kids!
Visit www.carolemarshmysteries.com to:

Join the Carole Marsh Mysteries Fan Club!

Write one sensational sentence using all five SAT
words in the glossary!

Download a Martian Word Search!

Take a Pop Quiz!

Download a Scavenger Hunt!

Learn Marvelous Mars Trivia!